~~Green~~ Janine
Goes to Foreign Parts.

by

Brian Tyrer

Illustrated by
John Bigwood

Seven Arches
Publishing

For Jane

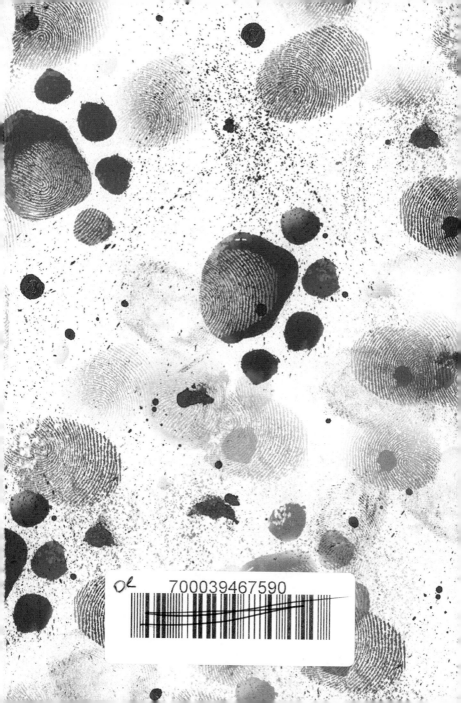

Published 2012 by Seven Arches Publishing
55, Countess Street, Stockport, SK2 6HB
www.sevenarchespublishing.co.uk

ISBN: 978-0-9567572-4-1

A catalogue record for this book is available from the
British Library

Graphics by Alan McGlynn

CHAPTER 1
Over to Dover

One morning Green Janine woke up and decided she was going to go cycling in foreign parts.

At that moment the dog walked into her bedroom.

"Hi dog," she said. "I'm going to go cycling in foreign parts today and you can come too if you like."

"What do you mean foreign parts?" asked the dog.

"Abroad of course, across the English Flannel, to France."

"Why France?" said the dog.

"Because that's nearest, and we can be back in time for tea," said Green Janine.

"I didn't know you could speak French," said the dog.

"What do you mean speak French?"

"You have to be able to speak French, or they won't be able to understand you."

"Hmmmm, I don't think my teacher is French," said Green Janine. "She says she doesn't understand me."

"French people speak a different language and you won't understand what they are saying to you."

"Well we can't let a little thing like that stop us can we?" said Green Janine.

"Here's another little thing then," said the dog. "You haven't got a passport."

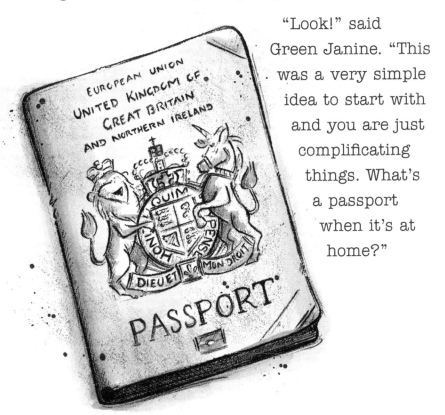

"Look!" said Green Janine. "This was a very simple idea to start with and you are just complificating things. What's a passport when it's at home?"

"Oh dear me,"
said the dog. "This is
going to be a difficult day."

"Never mind about that," said Green Janine,
"just tell me what a passport is."

"It's a little book with your photograph in it,
and it says who you are," replied the dog.

"But I know exactly who I am," said Green
Janine.

"Yes, but they won't in France," said the dog.

"And anyway, I do have one because I went to Florida when you and the cat went to the 'Daisy Hill Animal Farm' last year."

"Have you got a passport dog?" asked Green Janine.

"No and as it happens I have something else important to do anyway," said the dog.

"I'm going round to see my friend Maxwell."

"That Maxwell is a rough lot," said Green Janine.

"Not really, just because he's big doesn't mean he's rough," said the dog.

"Suit yourself," said Green Janine.

"If I'm lucky," said the dog and he left.

*m- *m- *m-

A moment later the cat walked in.

"Well cat," said Green Janine, "how about France?"

"How about France what?" said the cat.

"I'm going there for a bike ride, would you like to come with me?" said Green Janine.

"Not really," said the cat. "It's a nice day and I was counting on doing a lot of lying down in the sun."

"Mind you don't get sunburnt," said Green Janine.

"Cats don't," said the cat.

When Green Janine got downstairs she said to her mother that she (Green Janine that is) was off biking around France for the day.

"That's nice dear," said her mother. "You'll want a good breakfast then as it's rather a long way."

"Yes," said Green Janine. "Can you tell me what's the best way of getting there?"

"I'd go to Dover if I were you," said her mother.

"Dovers?" asked Green Janine. "Where's that?"

"It's just opposite France," said her mother. "You can hop on a boat and be over there in no time."

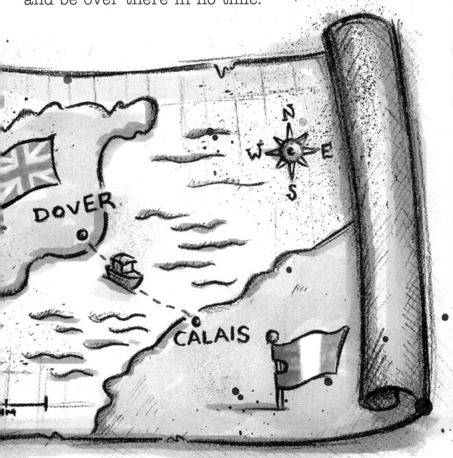

"Over from Dovers," said Green Janine. "Pity the dog won't come because it could have been over from Dovers with Rover."

"Yes," said her mother, "but the dog's not called Rover."

And so after a hearty breakfast of toast and kippers Green Janine made sure that she had her passport and a clean hanky.

She took out her bike and pumped up her tyres.

Green Janine wheeled her bike down the path towards the gate.

The dog appeared on the path in front of her.

Green Janine said, "Look dog, last chance - in the basket - no running like you usually do when we go **WALKIES**. I'll do all the pedalling and you can keep a sharp look out for poodles."

Just as she got to the gate there was a very colourful and enormous explosion followed by a strong smell of garlic.

When the dust had settled, there stood Mr. Mephista.

"Hmmm..." said Green Janine. "Suppose you wouldn't like to explain what you are doing dressed up like that?"

"Well, since we're going to France, I thought I would look the part. I'm supposed to be a traditional French onion seller."

"Don't they have supermarkets in France?" said Green Janine.

"Yes they do, but they call them 'supermarché'."

"You speak French then?" asked Green Janine.

"Oui, oui," said Mr Mephista.

"I can't believe you just said that," said Green Janine. "You should have gone before you came out."

"Oui means 'yes' in French," said Mr Mephista.

"YOU'VE GOT TO BE JOKING," said Green Janine.

CHAPTER 2
Not Happy with the Big Apple

"**H**ow are you going to get there then?" said Mr Mephista.

"Over from Dovers on a boat."

"There is another way," said Mr Mephista and he began to rotate more and more quickly.

There was a lot of smoke and it felt as though there was a big wind coming. Then all at once it seemed as if they were not where they had been a moment before.

"Fantabulous!" said Green Janine. "But, if I didn't know better, I'd say that was the Statue of Liberty."

"Y-es," said Mr Mephista.

"And if I didn't know better, I'd say that the Statue of Liberty is not in France. Isn't it in America?"

"Y-es again," said Mr Mephista, "but they do speak English, of a kind, in America."

"IT ISN'T FRANCE!" said Green Janine, "I had set my heart on going to France. You know I had."

One very apologetic explosion and a minute later they were standing in front of a very large tower.

"That's the Eiffel tower. It's named after Mr Eiffel so I can definitely say that we are now in France," said Mr Mephista.

"Are you sure it's not Blackpool Tower?" said Green Janine.

"Can you see the sea?" asked Mr Mephista.

"This is Paris but the French call it 'Pa-ree.' Paris is the most important town in France - it's the capital city."

"A bit like London then," said
Green Janine, "except that
London has the River Thames
going through it."

"Paris has the River Seine,"
said Mr Mephista. "We can go
on a boat trip down the river
if you like; it's a big river just
like the Thames."

"NO! I want to get on with my bike ride; it's a very healthy way of travelling you know."

They had not gone very far when a French
policeman jumped out
in front of them.

"'Ello, 'ello,
'ello" said the French
policeman. "You are in foreign parts, no?"

"I can speak French; I can understand every
word he says!" exclaimed Green Janine
excitedly.

"Isn't magic wonderful?" said Mr Mephista to no one in particular.

"I am in foreign parts, yes," said Green Janine.

"Well you 'ave to ride on the other side of the road 'ere like everyone else - or you will 'ave the accident," said the policeman. "You 'ave to ride on the right 'and side."

"Watch or bangle?" asked Green Janine.

"Watch," said the dog from the safety of the basket.

"TERRIFIC," said Green Janine to herself. "No one told me that foreign people ride on the wrong side of the road."

CHAPTER 3
Bon Appetite
(which is French for 'Enjoy your meal')

So they waved bye-bye to the policeman and set off cycling down the same side of the road as everyone else.

"I'm glad we got that sorted out," said Green Janine. "I wonder what else is different over here?"

While she was wondering, her stomach began to rumble.

"What do French people eat for lunch then?" she said to Mr Mephista.

"Park your bike outside here and we will find out," he replied.

They parked their bikes and went into the café. Inside there were tables covered with red and white check table cloths.

They ordered soup to start with and a bowl of water for the dog.

The dog was very pleased to see that French people were clearly dog lovers as many of them had brought their little dogs with them to eat in the café.

"No trouble, now dog," whispered Green Janine to the dog as he looked around.

"What are these black bits in this soup?" said Green Janine.

"They're escargots," said Mr Mephista.

"I quite like escrogits, they're a bit chewy but otherwise they're OK," said Green Janine. "What are they?"

¡?!¿?!¿?!

"Escargots are snails," said Mr Mephista.

"SNAILS! You're sitting there eating snails... and letting me eat snails!"

"I thought you said you liked them," said Mr Mephista.

"That was before I knew what they were," said Green Janine.

"I only hope they don't dish up the frogs legs then," murmured Mr Mephista.

To finish, they both had upside down apple pie.

"I need some exercise to work off that lunch," said Green Janine.

"Back on the bike then," said Mr Mephista.

CHAPTER 4:
A Yellow Jersey
(what's that when it's at home?)

"Which way?" said Green Janine.
"Turn left," shouted Mr Mephista.

"Watch or bangle?" shouted back Green Janine.

"Bangle," said the dog from inside the basket.

They hadn't gone far when Green Janine noticed that there were people lining the roads and they were cheering and waving as Green Janine and Mr Mephista rode along. The next minute a motorbike came alongside with a man sitting on the back holding a television camera.

Green Janine smiled sweetly at him thinking how nice it would be for her mother to see her on the television.

Just then Mr Mephista said **"OH NO!"** in a 'something is seriously wrong' sort of way.

"What's up?" asked Green Janine.

"Err, can you peddle a bit faster?" said Mr Mephista looking over his shoulder.

"Why's that?" said Green Janine.

"You see all those chaps on bikes behind us? Well, they're trying to catch us."

"No chance!" said Green Janine and off she went like a rocket, her little legs all of a blur.

Soon they came to the outskirts of a big town. The chasing cyclists had not caught them but now the crowds lining the streets were cheering and clapping.

Suddenly the dog started
shouting, "Poodle! Poodle!
Abandon ship!" and
leapt from the
basket landing
next to a
fluffy white
poodle with
a pink bow on
its head.

Green Janine nearly
braked violently but saw a
sign just ahead that said,
'Finish.' It didn't say 'finish' of
course, but it said something like
that in French. So she raced on.

"Just in time," said Green Janine to
herself. "I'm getting tired of these chaps
chasing me and I could do with a rest."

All at once photographers were taking her picture and people were making a lot of fuss.

Mr. Mephista turned up.

"Just tell me what's going on here will you?" said Green Janine. "I'm getting tired of being kissed by all these people."

"Well," said Mr Mephista, "you're famous now you've just won the Tour de France."

"Tour de France, Tour de France, what's that when it's at home?"

"It's a bike race," said Mr Mephista. "The French take their bike racing very seriously. You're a heroine of French cycling."

With that a man with a red, white and blue ribbon round his waist pulled a very large yellow jumper over her head and gave her a big bottle of champagne.

After that Green Janine had to stand on a stage with two of the other cyclists. A young French lady gave them each a large bouquet of flowers and Green Janine was pleased to see that hers was by far the largest.

Suddenly Green Janine remembered that the dog wasn't with her anymore. She called him and tried to get off the stage to look for him but they wouldn't let her.

Then the dog appeared looking very disappointed having had to walk the rest of the way back. What was worse was that the poodle only spoke French, and he couldn't understand a word that it said.

Green Janine, now wearing the Yellow Jumper, bent down and picked up the dog and everyone went: "Ahh." The photographers went wild and took loads and loads of pictures of Green Janine holding the dog.

Then the band played some tunes and the other two cyclists took turns to cry and look very happy at the same time. Green Janine thought the last tune was one she knew and so she decided that she had better cry and look very happy as well.

That was obviously the end of things so the crowd started to pack up and go home.

"Oh," said Green Janine, "it must be nearly teatime let's go home as well."

~~~ ~~~ ~~~

When they got home, Mr Mephista disappeared and Green Janine put her bike away and went into the house.

"How was France dear?" said her mother.

FANTABULOUS" said Green Janine. "They kiss you a lot, they ride bikes a lot on the wrong side of the road and I can't begin to tell you about some of the things they eat."

"I'll bet they don't have spaghetti on toast and Eccles cakes for tea," said her mother.

If you have enjoyed Green Janine's adventure in France, read about how she caught the two burly burglars, Bob and Bill in...

GREEN JANINE'S RULES FOR COLOURING IN HER PICTURES

This is not a rule. This is how you can get free colouring pages. Just go to the Competition page at **www.sevenarchespublishing.co.uk**

1. Always colour me in green and colour my hair in a different green.

2. Always colour my dress in purple or mauve.

3. If you haven't got a purple you can make it by mixing red and blue.

4. If you are good at colouring don't go over the lines. If you are not good at colouring, or are little, you can go over the lines a lot.

5. When you have finished all the pictures, you could put them together to make a book and enter our FABULOUSLY FABULOUS COMPETITION.

Just to let you know, I will not speak to anyone who colours my dress in PINK!!!!!!

FABULOUSLY FABULOUS COMPETITION

After you have downloaded the pictures from **www.sevenarchespublishing.co.uk** and coloured them in, you could make them into a book by stapling the pages together.

Books always have covers. If you design a FABULOUS cover for your book of coloured in pictures, you could win a prize in our book cover competition. Just take a photograph of your design for the cover, don't forget the title and the name of the author, that's you, and send the photograph to the email address:

admin@sevenarchespublishing.co.uk

What's the prize? you ask. Twenty-five wonderful English pounds to spend on whatever you like!

Is there a closing date? No. Just check the website on the competition page and if you can see your cover there, you know we will be sending you your prize. We can't get it to you unless a responsible adult such as your parent, carer, teacher or librarian puts their address on the email. That way we can send them the money and they can give it to you.

HAVE A GO!

A LITTLE CAT PUZZLE

The cat was tempted to go with Green Janine on her bike ride but then changed its mind. It decided to go its own way, as cats always do.

If you look carefully, you will see that the cat enjoys foreign travel just as much as Green Janine. How many times does the cat get into the picture? Turn this page upside down to see if you were right.

A BIG WORD PUZZLE

Did you notice that Green Janine sometimes gets words muddled up? Well we all do sometimes, I suppose, especially if we are speaking a foreign language, but perhaps some people do more often than others. This puzzle is simple. Just find out how many words Green Janine gets wrong and then see if you can write them down on a piece of paper spelt correctly. Turn this page upside down to see if you were right about the number.

The French policeman gets some words wrong as well, but that is a completely different matter so don't include the ones he gets wrong.

Answers: There are nine cats.
The number of words Green Janine gets wrong is five.

ABOUT THE AUTHOR

Brian Tyrer was born during the Second World War. He lives in Lewes in Sussex. Green Janine Goes to Foreign parts is the second book written by Brian about Green Janine that has been published. In a former life he was a teacher and then a school inspector.

Whilst teaching, the staff from his school met with Alex Brychta, the well-known illustrator for Oxford Reading Tree and they described him. This is the drawing he made from their description. It's an uncanny resemblance.

ABOUT THE ILLUSTRATOR

John Bigwood says he studied Art and Design at Bolton University and got a simply magnificent degree. He doesn't look old enough for that, but he must be because he is so good at drawing absolutely everything. He lives in London in a flat with his lovely girlfriend. His mum and dad live just round the corner and make sure he catches trains on time, and charges the battery in his mobile phone. Even so it is hard to contact him because he leaves it switched off almost always.

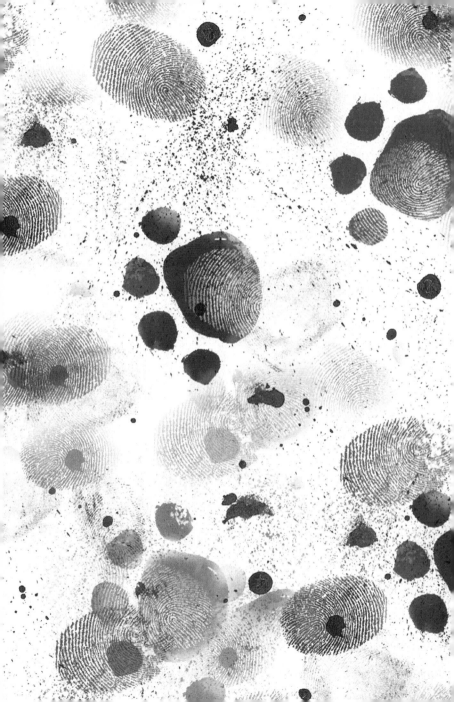